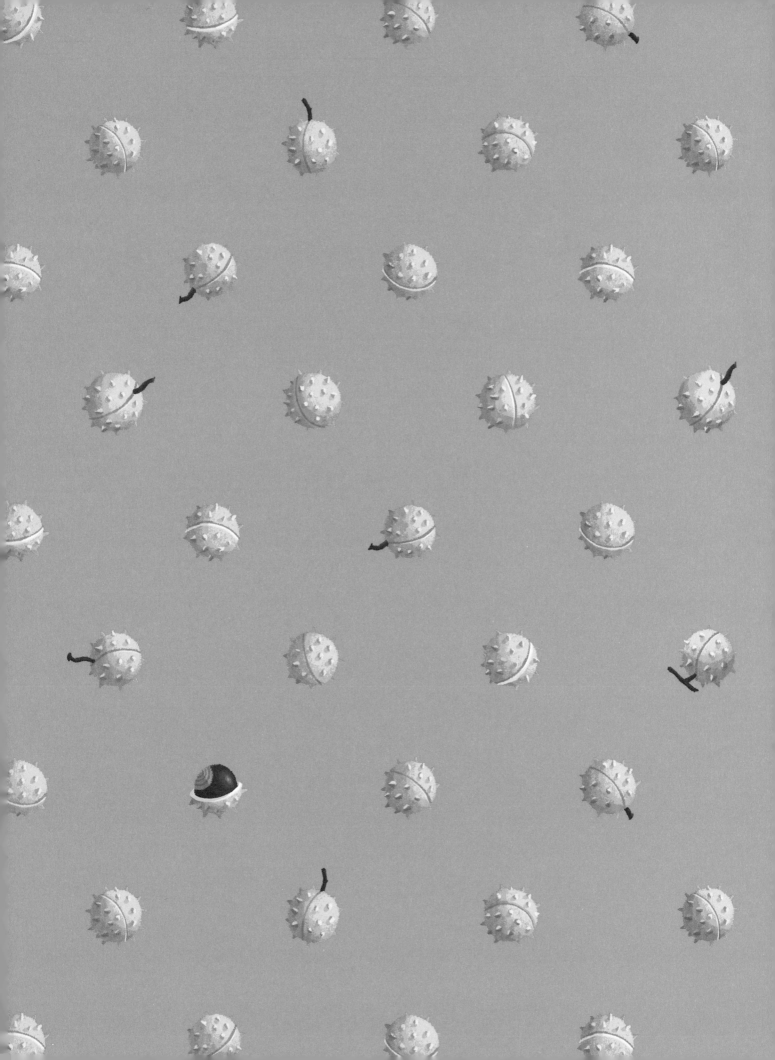

DOG
GONE

TEDDY

IF LOST, CALL
77-50854

For Tammy, Sacha and Ringo

DOG GONE

Written and illustrated by

Rob Biddulph

HarperCollins *Children's Books*

First published in hardback in Great Britain by
HarperCollins *Children's Books* in 2020

HarperCollins *Children's Books* is a division of HarperCollins*Publishers* Ltd.
Text and illustrations copyright © Rob Biddulph 2020
The author/illustrator asserts the moral right to be identified as the
author/illustrator of the work. A CIP catalogue record for this book
is available from the British Library. All rights reserved.

Visit our website at www.harpercollins.co.uk

ISBN: 978-0-00-831792-8
Printed and bound in China
1 3 5 7 9 8 6 4 2

FIVE THINGS TO FIND IN THIS BOOK

1. A blue glove ☐
2. A yellow submarine ☐
3. A pink kettle ☐
4. A black cat ☐
5. A rainbow ☐

BIRD-SPOTTING

Hidden in the pages of this book are a robin, a blue tit, five parakeets, a swan, a penguin, two pigeons, a heron,
a duck, three magpies (one for sorrow, two for joy) and a very shy owl. Can you spot them all?

I'm Edward Pugglesworth.
How do you do?

And this is the house
where I live with my crew.

There's
Foxy...

Lord
Squeakerton...

Hot Dog...

the Bears...

And Dave,
my pet human.
I keep him upstairs.

He's not too much trouble. He's tidy and neat.

He plays with his ball

and he eats
the odd treat.

I love my pet human.
He's loyal and true.
But sometimes I think that...

I should have got two.

And now for our story! I'll always remember
That crisp autumn day at the end of September.

I woke Dave at eight
with a "Good morning" bark,

And took him straight out
for his walk in the park.

The air cooled our breath
as we kicked through the leaves.

We bumped into Shadow...

We said hi to Jeeves...

We nodded to Heron...

gave Rabbit a wave...

And then we both froze and I hid behind Dave.

For there in the shed by the merry-go-round
They say that a TERRIBLE TROLL can be found.

With fur-covered face and huge eyes of bright green,
He loves chasing dogs with his

EATING MACHINE!

My heart was a-flutter,
a leaf on the breeze,
As we crept past the shed
and the dark, twisted trees.

And then we both ran
just as fast as we could,
And we didn't stop running
till Cherry Tree Wood.

Relieved, we decided to play with Dave's ball,
And that's when we noticed the rain start to fall.

A rumble of thunder... The wind gathered speed...
"It's home-time!" I woofed, and put Dave on his lead.

We set off at pace, but the storm came in fast.
And then, by the bench, I felt something zoom past:

Two squirrels, a flurry of grey, white and black.
"Your acorns!" I shouted. "You've dropped them! Come back!"

I picked up the nuts and began to give chase.
I flew through those woods like a rocket through space.

Alas, I could not catch that squirrelly pair,
So I turned to my human...

...but Dave wasn't there!

I retraced my steps.
Where on earth did he go?

I bumped into Heron,
but she didn't know.

And neither did Rabbit.
He hadn't a clue.

I'd lost my pet human!
What was I to do?

I ran to the bandstand...

I circled the pond...

I looked through the wood...

and the meadow beyond.

Finally, with a cold feeling of dread,
I went back to check out the

SCARY TROLL SHED!

I pushed with my nose and the door opened wide.
I took a deep breath and I tiptoed inside.

And there in the darkness, an awful surprise!
For looking straight at me were...

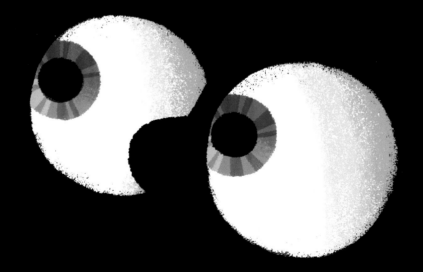

...TWO BRIGHT GREEN EYES!

My hackles shot up and with trembling knees
I ran from the shed through the dark, twisted trees.

I zigged and I zagged – I could hear him behind me.
I needed to hide where the troll wouldn't find me.

But then... a dead end! I was trapped in between
The fence and the terrible eating machine.

My legs turned to jelly. My thoughts were a muddle.
And then the troll grabbed me and gave me...

...a cuddle!

"Hello there," he said. "What a handsome young fellow.
I've seen you before, with that chap dressed in yellow.

Oh dear. Have you lost him? Well, that just won't do.
Fear not, little doggy! I'll find him for you."

We rode his machine to the place that sells tea,
And there was my human as safe as could be.

A whirlwind
of huggles
and licks
and embraces...

Kindness.

It's found in the
strangest of places.

And so, dearest reader, our story ends here.
A day of adventure, new friendships and cheer.

Have fun in the park, but I do recommend
That you keep a close eye...

...on your two-legged friend.

THE END

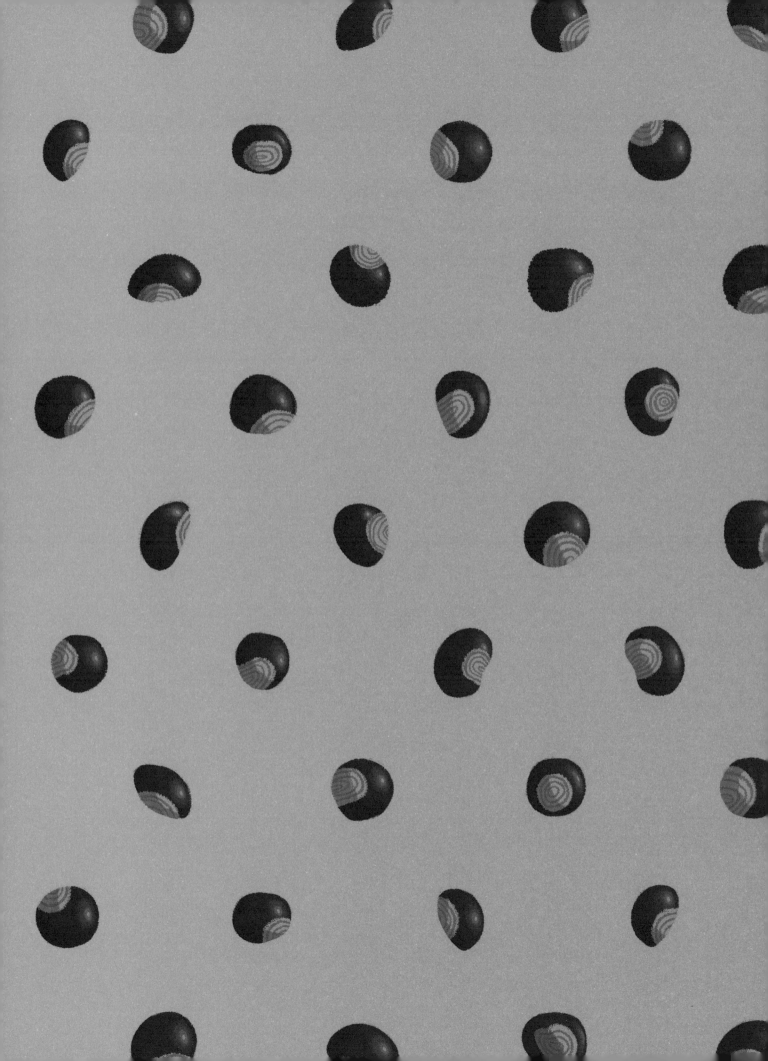

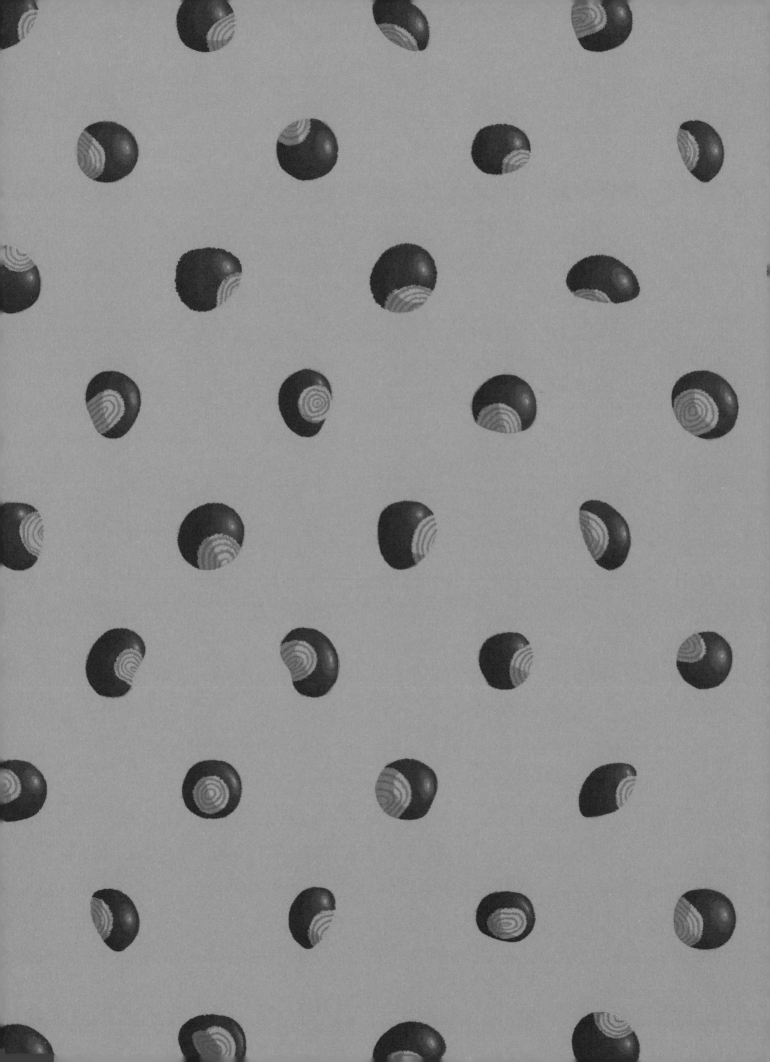